SHATTERED GLASS

Patrick Gloutney

To all those and their families who suffer from the constant struggle of depression.

"We are not defined by what tragedy does to us but rather what we do with it."

Gabe Ledford twirled his lucky bullet between his fingers as he walked down the street. This bullet had saved his life before by misfiring, but it wouldn't work this time. That was a dark day for Gabe, it seemed as though not even the gun would be nice to him. No one had. Similar to his previous attempt, Gabe was taking one last walk around, but unlike last time, he had a letter that he had to deliver. The letter was not one of anger, but rather, love. When he reached the house of the girl of his dreams, he slipped it into the mailbox, sighed and walked on.

Why bother, he thought to himself. *Let her carry the damn burden. She deserves it after all.* Deep down, though, Gabe knew he couldn't do that to her, and that's why he had written the letter.

Gabe walked through his front door about half an hour later. His parents weren't home, like always, so it was easy for him to grab a glass of whiskey.

He had never had whiskey before, but he hoped it would help to take the edge off what he was going to do. He walked downstairs and grabbed the keys to his father's gun case. He gently opened the door and pulled the .22 calibre handgun from its place. He locked up the case and walked to his room. There he sat, just looking at the gun sitting on his desk, for what felt like hours. The half-full glass of whiskey beside it.

Just do it already, you idiot, he thought. *No one cares, and no one will. You'll be the laughing stock of the school if you go back.* He reached for the gun, but something was stopping him, and he couldn't figure out what. He had no real friends except one, and that guy would be better off without him. This thought seemed to help. The world would be better without him. No one would have to go out of their way to protect him, and those who picked on him would be able to find someone else; hell, they may even stop altogether. He glanced at the picture of his dream girl on his desk, and the memories of the things she had done to him came flooding back. With that, Gabe grabbed the gun and whiskey. He placed the gun's barrel to his temple and downed the last of his drink. As the burning liquid flowed into his stomach, he pulled the trigger. His glass shattered as it hit the floor a second later.

Brian walked up the steps to Gabe's house. The poor kid had had a horrible day. The worst Brian had ever seen. He had known Gabe for ages and saw his descent into depression. He had worked hard to try and keep Gabe afloat, but it was getting harder and much more demanding. However, that didn't matter. He was worried that Gabe would try something tonight, and he wanted to make sure that it wasn't successful.

"Gabe you all right? It's me, Brian," he called as he knocked on the door. There was no answer. "C'mon man, I'm worried about you." Brian hit the door frame in frustration, walked down onto the lawn and looked up at Gabe's window. What he saw made his heart skip. The window was shattered. Brian ran to the door and forced it open. He ran upstairs and threw Gabe's bedroom door open. What he saw made him gag and choke back tears.

"Gabe," he whispered. Brian slowly approached the lifeless body that was once his friend. He saw the shattered glass on the floor and couldn't hold back his tears. They fell, making wet streaks down his face.

"I could have helped you through this," he sobbed. "If you had only waited a little longer." He began to kick himself for stopping for gas on the way over. If he had only been here sooner, he might have been able to save Gabe's life. He noted the way Gabe was seated. Laying face down on the desk, his hair a mess of blood and brain matter, his skull gapping open from the exit wound of the bullet, a lifeless hand laying on top of the .22 on the desk and the blood-covered picture of José to his left, the girl who had humiliated Gabe at school just a few hours before. With shaking hands, Brian pulled out his cell phone and dialled Gabe's mother's cell. His father was away on business, so there was no point in calling him. He heard her answer and didn't wait for a hello.

"I couldn't stop him...," he sobbed.

"Who is this?"

"I'm here right now in his room. He had a rough day, and I guess...you should come home. Gabe's..." Brian stopped as he felt a lump forming in his throat. "...d...dead."

"What?" he heard a faint voice answer after a long pause that felt like an eternity for Brian. He heard a reply, "I...I just saw him this morning...He was...no...or was it homework?" There was another long pause as the rambling died off. "I'll be right home." With that, she hung up. Brian took one last look at his friend and then headed downstairs. He headed straight out the door. He couldn't stay in the house any longer. He made it to his car before he broke down.

"Hey Mom," José called as she walked in.

"Hello, dear, how was your day?" her mother asked absentmindedly as she watched the news.

"Not bad, yours?"

"Same. There's a letter for you on the counter," Her mother informed her. José said her thanks and walked to the kitchen. She grabbed the letter; it smelled of lilacs. As she opened it, a gold chain with a circle of a fifth pendant on it fell out. She smiled. Whoever sent this knew how much she loved music. She had never seen a pendant like this. The circle of fifths was a tool used to determine the number of sharps and flats in each key. It was simultaneously a music student's best friend and worst nightmare. She had never seen it converted into jewelry and couldn't imagine how hard it would have been to find. She placed the chain on the counter and read the letter.

Dear José,

I don't know why you did what you did today. But I decided that it was time I tell you how I feel. I fell in love with you a long time ago, but never had the courage to approach you about it. I had thought, up until now, that you had no leanings in regards to your opinion of me. Today I realized that was not true. Although I hate what you've done to me, I do not hate you.

Please accept this pendant as a reminder of me. I know how much you love music, so I thought this could be a nice piece of jewelry as well as help you with your studies.

I will love you always, even if you don't love me back.
Sincerely,
Gabe.

José sat down, stunned. She had just manipulated and humiliated this kid, and he gives her jewelry? It didn't make sense. She had no idea that he had feelings for her, let alone that they would last through what she had done as a prank. She felt horrible now. She would make it up to him tomorrow. She got up and put the necklace around her neck. As she walked to the bathroom to see how it looked, she saw something that made her stop dead in her tracks. On the television screen was the heading: *Teenage Boy Commits Suicide,* and above the headline was a picture of Gabe's house. She let the lilac-scented letter fall from her grasp.

"Oh my god," she whispered as she slowly walked into the living room.

"Such a waste, don't you think?" her mother asked when she noticed her. José didn't respond. She just kept staring at the screen. "You, okay?" her mother asked.

"I...I know that house."

Brian handed Gabe's mother a tissue and then turned back to the police, barely keeping it together himself. It was bad enough that Gabe was gone, but now the local news was set up outside, trying to pry whatever information they could from the neighbours. It was sickening. They cared only for their story and ratings, and nothing about those affected.

"So, you say that you were coming to visit Gabe? May I ask why?" the officer asked.

"He had a rough day at school. I knew his parents wouldn't be home, so I decided to come and make sure he was all right. I was...I was trying to prevent something like this." Brian explained working hard to suppress his feelings.

"You had reason to think this would happen?"

"Yes. Gabe had tried to take his life once before, about six months ago, after an argument with his parents. The only thing that saved him was a misfire on the gun he used. After that day, he always carried that dud bullet around with him for good luck."

"That will be all. Thank you for your time," the officer said and left. Brian sat down next to Gabe's mother.

"Walter is on his way," she said between her sobs. Brian nodded but said nothing. It was still kind of surreal to him. "Thank you for calling me."

"I should have been here sooner."

"Don't say that. You came, and that's all that matters. Heaven knows I should have been here rather than at work," Gabe's mother stated.

"You couldn't have known," Brian responded. There was a long moment of silence before they heard the stretcher being carried down the stairs.

"You said there was a broken glass?" Gabe's mom asked.

Brian was caught off guard by the question, but responded. "Yah...I don't know why he had it, though."

Gabe's mother sighed. "There was a whiskey bottle on the counter. He must have used it to make it easier."

"I should be getting home. My mother will be worried sick," Brian said, shaking his head. "I imagine that she'll be over before long," Brian got up, but Gabe's mother grabbed his arm.

"If you see the bitch that caused this, do me a favour, will you?"

"Whatever you need."

"Deck her."

José walked down the school hallway in more of a trance than anything. She hadn't been able to focus during her first two classes, and she certainly wasn't herself.

When she opened her locker, she smashed herself in the face with the door hard enough to hurt her jaw and cause her to drop all her books and papers. She knelt to pick them up, tears welling in her eyes. Nothing was going right today. Nothing had been going right since she heard about Gabe. She still couldn't believe it.

Was it because of me? She asked herself. *Of course, it was because of you. No. There must have been more. Right? One person can't cause something like this, can they? There had to be more.* Deep down, though, she knew her prank had killed him. She never should have agreed to do it; she should have let someone else seduce him.

Her phone beeped just as she finished sorting her papers. She looked at it. It was a text from her best friend. It was the video of the prank they had pulled. She didn't even look at it, she just deleted it.

"You need some help?" José looked up to see the friend who had sent her the text.

"Nah, I've got Adriana."

"You alright? You haven't been yourself today, and what happened to your jaw?" Adriana remarked. José gingerly touched her jaw, it was beginning to swell from its earlier contact with the locker, and she had only just realized the pain.

"Just thinking. We never should have pulled that prank yesterday," José responded, brushing off the question about her jaw.

"Ah, it was all in good fun. Besides, the guy's a total nerd," Adriana stated, flipping her hair back, evidently oblivious to what had happened, "Nice necklace by the way."

"Oh, thanks, it was a gift..." José stopped herself. She knew that if she dwelt on this subject that it would make her cry. Just as she was about to say something, she heard someone call out.

"You little bitch!" José looked to see Gabe's friend, Brian.

"He's dead because of you!"

"Hey, lay off, buster!" Adriana yelled.

The tears in José's eyes fell. She scrambled to her feet and closed her locker door. "I know," she whispered. She ran to the stairwell, then outside and in the frigid fall air, she sat under a tree and cried. She felt the pendant shift under her shirt, which only made her cry harder. She quickly grabbed it, ripping it off her neck. She didn't deserve it, but at the same time, she couldn't bring herself to throw it away; instead, she placed it in her pocket. Why? Why did she have to be so cruel to the poor guy? If not for her, Gabe would still be alive. Her jaw was beginning to hurt, and she was shivering when she heard footsteps. She looked up and saw Brian, his hand in a fist.

"Why?" he demanded, "Why did you have to do it?"

"I don't know," José sobbed, "It was supposed to be funny...It was never meant to hurt him."

"You didn't think, that's what happened. You stupid, arrogant bitch, you and all your friends." Brian yelled.

"I know...I know. I'm sorry," José cried.

"Sorry doesn't bring him back," Brian snapped, "Here." He handed her a piece of ice wrapped in cloth and pointed to her jaw.

"Thank you," she stated softly, and tentatively touched the ice to her swelling cheek.

"He really loved you. You know that, right?" Brian asked, his tone softening.

"I do now," she responded, pulling the pendant from under her shirt, "He sent me this yesterday."

"Get inside. The last thing we need around here is another death."

Patrick Gloutney

6

Brian walked down the hallway. He was angry and confused, but most of all, he was sad. He was torn up by the death of his best friend, but he was even more upset with himself for yelling at José. As much as he wanted to, he couldn't justify it, no matter how hard he tried. There was no way whatsoever that she could have known what her little joke was going to do. She still shouldn't have pulled it anyway, but he could start to see how her ignorance would allow her to think it was justified.

It was the end of the day, and he had planned to get his stuff, jump in his car and drive over to check on Gabe's parents. He felt sorrier for them than anyone. He could imagine what losing your son would be like if this is how he felt about losing a friend. He never made it to his car, though. He noticed a couple of the guys José usually hung out with loitering in the parking lot. He was halfway across the lot when they called out. Brian tried to ignore them, but they were persistent.

"Hey dimwit! Can you hear me?" one yelled as he grabbed Brian's arm. Brian turned to face them and was met by a fist to the face. He staggered back, dropping his books.

"How's that feel? You like beating up on girls, you should be able to take a few," and with that, Brian received another punch, this time to his gut. The assailant's fist hit his keys, and the panic alarm on his car began to blare. His attackers didn't care. The one who had done all the talking grabbed him by the collar of his shirt.

"What do you think you're doing, embarrassing my girl?"

"I was unaware she was dating anyone," Brian spat.

"Not at the moment. But she'll come around," the jock snapped.

"Mr. Harrison. Put that young man down," Brian heard the familiar voice of his English teacher. The jock holding Brian glanced to his left and then let Brian fall to the ground.

"You can't just go around attacking people. Is this what you do instead of studying for my tests? Might explain some things," the teacher added.

"No sir," the jock responded.

"Off with you then," the teacher stated, and the jocks scampered off. "That goes for you to young lad." Brian nodded and picked up his things.

"Thank you," he mumbled and loaded this stuff into the trunk of his Honda Civic.

"How are you doing?" the teacher asked as Brian climbed into the driver's seat.

"I'm fine," Brian lied and started his car.

José gently rested her fingers on the keys of the piano in front of her. She had come in early and found the music teacher caught up in preparations for the concert band. But José sat, trying to play but not able to. She managed to play D minor, then started to sob.

Stupid idiot, she thought, *play the saddest chord you know.* She slowly began to play a scale to warm up, then she began to play around in the key of D minor. Then she changed to C. Satisfied, she got up and grabbed a blank score. As she sat back down, she felt the weight of her pendant press against her breast. She slowly took it off and set it on the stand where she could clearly see it. She had debated what to do with the pendant for hours. At first, it was unbearable for her to wear but she had eventually decided she needed to wear it. It was what Gabe would have wanted. It would also serve as a reminder to her to treat others fairly and hopefully prevent her from being such a naïve idiot in the future. Of course, she had needed to repair the clasp from when she ripped it from her neck the day before, but it was time well spent. Who needs to pass a chemistry test anyway?

She took a shaky breath and started to play a melody that had been in her head since Brian had chastised her. It was the melody to *That Girl* by Jordan McIntosh. After getting more confident with it and putting some notes on staff paper so she could write out a piano part, she began to hum and then softly sing a parody.

> *That boy...he had a beautiful heart that I shattered like glass*
> *That boy is still in love with me. Mmm...*
> *If I could, I'd erase every teardrop stain I left on his face*
> *Sometimes I wish I'd never known...that boy.*
> *Gotta know where I'm coming from.*
> *I was the bullet coming out of his gun.*
> *What I did...*

Jessie slammed the keys hard enough to startle the music teacher. She caught an angry glance, but the old woman said nothing. Jessie wiped a tear from her eye. What she had sung was true, but it didn't sound right. Another tear fell as she wrote more lyrics down. She then played around with the notes a little to fit them better. When she was done, she was satisfied but didn't dare try singing it again for fear of breaking down.

"I've never actually heard you play." José jumped and turned around to find Brian standing in the doorway. "It sounds nice."

"I was just playing around," José responded. "You know any instruments?"

"Drums. Nothing fancy, though. Wouldn't even say I'm that good," Brian responded.

"I'd love to hear you sometime," José noticed a flash of something in Brian's eyes.

"Gabe wanted me to enter the talent competition," he said, his voice sounding distant. There was a long moment of silence before Brian spoke again. "About yesterday. I shouldn't have yelled at you."

"I deserved it. I was so stupid," José said, glancing at the pendant on the piano stand.

"You were," Brian stated bluntly, "but there was no way you could have predicted the outcome."

José's frown deepened. "Why did he never say anything to me?" she asked, "He was cute enough. I mean, I would have at least given it a shot."

"You say that now. But would you have said that a couple of days ago?" Brian's answer.

José sighed. She hated herself for the truth behind the answer to that question. She wouldn't have. He was just a nerd; no way she was going to date a nerd. Looking back at it now, though, she had been foolish and close-minded.

"Exactly," Brian said as he turned to leave, his voice as cold as ice.

"You doing anything at lunch?" José called after him. Brian raised an eyebrow at her, "I'm writing a song and I'd like to see what a drummer could bring to it."

"Maybe another time." The meaning behind Brian's words was all too clear: *I don't fault you, but I still blame you.*

Patrick Gloutney

Brian sighed heavily and stared at his textbook. His English teacher may have saved him from those jocks, but there was nothing he could do about Brian's current inability to retain information. They had just run through something and were given questions, but Brian couldn't remember a thing for the life of him. He finally gave up and opened up his computer, pretending to review his notes that he "made" earlier.

He accessed his picture file and began to scroll through pictures of him and Gabe. He stopped and enlarged the image of him and Gabe sitting behind Brian's drum set. Gabe had wanted so badly to know how to play an instrument to have a reason to talk with José. Unfortunately, Gabe wouldn't have been able to grasp an instrument if the world ended. Brian smiled, remembering how happy Gabe had been when he was able to tap out a basic rhythm on the snare drum.

Brian clicked to the next picture and almost laughed. It was a picture of him and Gabe bent over the hood of his Honda Civic, arguing. Even though Gabe was considered a nerd, he knew his way around an engine almost as much as Brian did. That particular day, they had been discussing how to modify the little black car into something more interesting. Brian was thinking Turbo Charger, a cool paint job, bigger tires and maybe a lift kit. Gabe, on the other hand, was the complete opposite. He was thinking of dropping it low, tweaking the engine a little and filling the car with a bunch of sensors relaying data to a computer that could change engine and car parameters to get the best mileage.

"I see you're very interested in Hamlet," Mr. Wright commented. Brian didn't even jump. He minimized the window and closed his computer.

"Sorry sir," he muttered and turned back to his work.

Mr. Wright tapped him on the shoulder and motioned for him to step outside. "You ready to tell me what's bothering you?" he asked, once they were in the hall.

"I told you I'm fine."

"You screamed at a young lady in the hallway; you got beaten up by a bunch of students in the parking lot, and now I catch you looking at photos of you and Gabe in my class rather than doing your work. I'll ask again, do you want to talk about it?"

Brian took a shaky breath. He knew this teacher well; he knew he could be open about how he felt, but he didn't want to. So, he just looked at the floor.

"Look, I know you and Gabe were close. But you can't let this thing drag you down."

"Gabe was more than a thing!" Brian snapped.

Mr. Wright put a hand on Brian's shoulder. "You're right. How improper of me. But how do you think he would feel if you were slipping in your classes because of him?"

"I'm not slipping," Brian stated defensively. He understood Mr. Wright's point, though. If he continued like this, his grade certainly would suffer. That would be the last thing that Gabe would have wanted. "I just can't focus."

"Then let me help you. Go get your work and bring it out here. We'll work through that together, and then I'm going to make you an appointment with Guidance," Mr. Wright said. Brian did as he was told.

It was nice to know that someone was willing to help him. He had been putting on a strong front for Gabe's parents and at school. He didn't really have anywhere but his room to let his feelings out, and recently, he had barely been home.

He sat next to Mr. Wright on the bench in the hall. Then the man said something that changed Brian's outlook on his whole situation.

"We are not defined by what tragedy does to us, but rather what we do with it."

Patrick Gloutney

José sat in her car, her hands still on the ignition key. She didn't know how long she had been sitting here, but it had been long enough for her mom's car to cool off.

This was a bad idea, she thought to herself. There was no way she could face Gabe's parents, and no way that they would ever forgive her. She should never have come. This thought had run through her head multiple times, but something was stopping her from turning the key. She knew she would have to do this eventually, but she was still scared to do it. Then she saw a black Honda Civic pull into the laneway. She swallowed hard as Brian climbed out and made his way to the back of the house. Then a red sports car pulled in next to the Honda Civic. José shook her head and finally pulled the key from her ignition. She climbed out and walked to the front porch. She stopped at the door.

No going back now, she thought, guilt and sadness turning inside her. She knocked, and a sad woman opened the door. The woman's mascara had run down her face, and her eyes were still wet with tears.

"Yes?" she asked with a trembling voice.

"José? What are you doing here?" Brian asked from behind the woman.

"I...I came to apologize," she managed. Brian nodded.

"If you need anything, Beth, I'll be out in the garage." With that, Brian was gone.

"Come in," Beth invited. José followed Beth to the living room, where they sat on the couch. "Now what exactly do you have to apologize for?"

"I'm the one...that pushed Gabe over the edge," José blurted out, and immediately kicked herself for saying it. The expression on Beth's face changed drastically.

"He died with your picture in front of him, you know," Beth stated coldly. There was a long moment of silence before José responded.

"He sent me this. I thought you'd like it back." José took the pendant from around her neck and, with a tear running down her face, placed it on the table. "I'm so sorry for every part I played. I was stupid and inconsiderate. I only hope that you don't blame yourself."

"Where is she?" someone shouted angrily from down the hall. Sure enough, Gabe's father walked into the room seconds later. "You know what you've done!" he shouted at her.

"Honey, I'm sure she doesn't need-"

"I'm very sorry, sir. I'll see myself out." José said, trying not to tremble. She stood up and left. Once in her car, she turned the key. The engine turned over sluggishly, and the lights on her display panel dimmed too barely on. At that moment, she realized the electrical system had been on the entire time she had been sitting at the curb. She rested her head on the steering wheel and started to cry.

Shouldn't have done that, she thought to herself: the anger in Gabe's father's eyes, the sadness in those of his mother, they were both mourning, and she had only made things harder. After a few minutes of wetting the steering wheel and making her makeup run, she popped the hood of her car and climbed back out. She was staring at the foreign object under the hood when she felt a hand grip her shoulder and spin her around.

"Don't ever give this away," Brian stated firmly, pressing the circle of fifths pendant into José's hand. "He gave it to you for a reason." José couldn't speak. She just nodded. Then Brian did something she didn't expect. He reached up and brushed a tear from her cheek. He sighed and pulled a rag from his pocket.

"You look like a monster," he muttered. With that, he began to gently wipe the smeared makeup off José's face. The cloth was cold and rough, but his touch wasn't. When he finished, he placed the cloth on the engine of her car.

"Gabe always did like you better without your makeup on," he said and cleaned off her battery with one hand, "Need a boost?"

"If you could," José said cautiously.

"I'll go grab my Honda." It took Brian less than five minutes to get the engine running again. José nodded her thanks and climbed into her car. Brian caught the door before it closed, rolled the window down and then shut the door.

"You mentioned a song?" he asked, leaning on the car. José was completely bewildered. This was the last thing she had expected. When she discovered she had drained her battery, she thought she'd be walking home, and now he wanted to discuss something that she thought was completely off the table.

"Yah...well, it's sort of a parody...I don't really know, I have changed a couple of words so far," she fumbled.

Brian just laughed. "When would you be working on it again?"

"Next Lunch. Probably before school as well," José answered. There was a moment of silence before she added. "I'm truly sorry for what I did. I hope you know that I don't ever expect your forgiveness. You don't have to be nice; you can hate me and never speak to me again if you prefer."

Brian shook his head. "Like I said before. There was no way you could have known. Besides, Gabe would shoot me if he saw me mad at you," Brian responded. José raised an eyebrow. "The only time he ever punched me was when I said that you were a worthless bitch and that he would be better off looking for someone else. He wouldn't stand for hearing anything bad about you."

Another tear fell from José's eye. That was so sweet. She wished now more than ever that she had had a chance to get to know Gabe better.

"I'll see you at lunch," Brian said and walked back to the house.

José drove down the street, crying and smiling at the fact that someone had cared that much for her, even when she had never treated him well. Then the guilt hit her like a brick wall.

José was surprised to find Brian sitting at the piano when she walked in at lunch. She hadn't expected him to actually come.

"Something wrong?" he asked. José slowly shook her head and placed her bag on a nearby chair. She pulled out her notebook and placed it on the stand by the piano.

"I was thinking I could play my part and then you could try and fit something in with the drums," she said, sort of distracted. Since yesterday, she hadn't been able to get him out of her head. There was something weird about it. He had been nice to her even though she was at fault for Gabe's death. Then again, Gabe had sent her the pendant after she had humiliated him. The whole thing scared José. She didn't want to have a guy stuck in her mind. It was bad enough that Gabe was there, but she certainly couldn't bear having Brian in there with him.

"Sounds like a plan to me," Brian said, pulling José from her thoughts.

José placed her fingers over the keys and hesitated slightly. What if he didn't like the song? What if he saw the true meaning of writing the parody? Why did it even matter? She pushed herself to play, not wanting to keep Brian waiting. He listened for a few verses, then stopped her. José looked at him worried.

"Do you have the lyrics?" he asked. José tentatively handed them to him. He reviewed them and then looked at her, his eyes wide with surprise.

"You rewrote it to apply to Gabe," he said distantly.

José nodded, thinking back to when she rewrote it a few days back. How sad she felt, how much she blamed herself, how much she still blamed herself.

"We have to talk right now about this," Brian stated harshly.

José winced slightly. "What...what do you mean?"

"This song blames you completely for his death. You can't keep thinking that," Brian explained, his tone softening.

"But I am-"

"No. You're not. You may have pulled that prank, but Gabe pulled the trigger. You didn't kill him; I didn't kill him. He killed himself. And don't flatter yourself by thinking it was solely because of you, because I can guarantee that there was more..." Brian stopped when José started to cry. They sat there for a few minutes with José sobbing. Brian glanced at the music teacher who was walking towards them. He held up a hand, and the teacher understood. She disappeared into her office.

"José, I didn't mean to—"

"Thank you." José said, cutting him off, "I needed to hear that." Then José did something that surprised even her. She leaned in and hugged Brian and gave him a kiss on the cheek. "You're a great guy." Brian must have been taken aback by this because he had no immediate response. He just looked at the lyrics.

"There are some more things that need changing, but I just can't fit words into it," José informed him, breaking the silence.

"What if it was a duet?" Brian asked. José raised an eyebrow.

"I can't sing very well, but what if it was sung from both perspectives?" Brian suggested. José smiled slightly. She hadn't considered that, but it was a great idea.

"I'm sure you can sing better than you let on," she commented, taking the notebook back and making a few notes. "Try singing this with the piano," she instructed after handing the notebook back to Brian.

Brian sighed and came in when cued.

"He was like a brother to me,
Like a member of the family
Staying over on Friday Nights
Yeah
But every time I look at you now
All I see is you blaming yourself
On the day his world came crashing down"

José stared at Brian, her mouth hung open. He had the most beautiful voice she and ever heard. She grabbed the notebook and looked at what she had written in disbelief. He had thrown in things she hadn't changed. She quickly grabbed her pencil and wrote down his version before she forgot.

"That bad, eh?" Brian asked.

"You kidding? That was perfect! More than perfect. I can't believe you think you can't sing," José replied.

"How long would this take to perfect?" Brian asked.

"I don't know, it depends on how much we work on it," José replied absentmindedly. She scribbled more notes down. Brian had given her an idea, and she wanted to get it down on paper.

"Could it be ready for the talent show coming up?" Brian inquired. José looked up, a little stunned.

"If we really work at it. You want to perform it?"

"Gabe wanted me to go in as a drummer anyway. I think it would be a nice tribute to him." Brian explained.

"Oh, Brian, that's so sweet. If we perform this, you have to sing, though," José stated.

Brian smiled, "I can live with that."

José pulled up to the curb outside Brian's house. She rubbed the pendant Gabe had given her between her fingers and shut off the ignition, making sure to turn it all the way off this time. She was beginning to have second thoughts about what she was about to do.

There was the school Christmas dance coming up, and she wanted to go, but not with just anyone. She wanted to go with Brian. When she first realized she had feelings for him, she kicked herself. But as they worked on their song over the last month, she had begun to fall in love with his voice and then the way he acted. When they worked together, she never once felt as if he was blaming her anymore, only that he understood her.

She found herself sneaking "Good Bye" hugs just to feel his warm embrace. As time drew on, she was able to channel the feelings into her work, but now she wanted more. She knew that Brian would never ask her to the dance for fear of dishonouring his best friend's memory, so José was going to ask him.

She climbed out of her car and walked to the door, her confidence fading slightly, worrying what he might think or say. She rang the doorbell, and Brian opened it.

"José? You alright?" he asked.

"Fine, I...uhm..." *Damn it!* She thought to herself. She had rehearsed this a thousand times, and now all her scripted words had just flown out the window.

"Did you want to work on the song? I have a drum kit here, and I don't have anything else planned. We could play the piano soundtrack through my computer." Brian suggested. José couldn't believe herself. All the confidence she had in the car was gone, every bit of it.

When she didn't respond for a few moments, Brian asked, "Are you sure you're okay?"

José shook herself out of her trance. "Perfectly fine," she responded, "I was thinking about the song and what if we did like a loop thing, layering various tracks of different instruments to get more depth out of it." She lied.

"I suppose we could try it. Do you have a looper or whatever they're called?"

"In my car," José responded, *I think.* Brian nodded, and José made her way back to her car, popping the trunk.

You stupid idiot! What the hell happened back there? She asked herself. She rummaged through her trunk and realized that she did, in fact, have a looping board. She muttered her thanks and brought it into the house.

Brian's room was rather messy with sports clothing strewn on the floor, and he had to pull a few shirts off the cymbal on his drum kit. "Sorry about the mess. I wasn't expecting company," Brian commented, picking up yet more clothing from the floor. José smiled.

"Brian, who was at the door?" José heard a female voice ask.

"It's José, the girl from school I have been working on that song with," Brian called back. José saw a blond-haired woman poke her head around the corner. José lifted her hand in a wave, and the blond smiled.

"Alright. You two have fun. The door stays open, though," the woman commented and disappeared.

"Geez, Mom," Brian muttered, "Sorry about that."

"It's fine," José responded.

"So, what were you thinking of looping?"

José felt her heart rate pick up a little. She had no idea. She supposed a guitar would be nice, but there wasn't one around, maybe a second drum part, but the one they had now sounded so good on its own. José clutched the box she was holding a little tight, hoping somehow it would give her an answer.

"Can I have a hug?" she blurted out. Brian raised an eyebrow.

"Yeah, sure. What's wrong?" he asked, taking the box from her and placing his arms around her. José rested her head on his shoulder, a smile spreading across her lips. His embrace was so gentle, so comforting. She felt her confidence coming back.

"You didn't come here to work on the song, did you?" José looked at him, a little surprised.

"Why would you say that?"

"Because the box you were holding is empty." José watched as Brian opened it, showing her the vacancy inside.

You are such an idiot, she said to herself.

"What's on your mind?"

José took a deep breath and sighed heavily. "Will you go to the dance with me?" she asked. Brian blinked, looking at her, stunned. He let go of her and took a seat at his drum kit.

"José...I didn't mean to lead you on or anything—"

"You didn't. No, you never indicated any hint of wanting a relationship, but I want one. Your drumming is exemplary, voice, incredible, you're incredible," José could feel herself beginning to babble, but she didn't want him to say no.

"You know I can't," Brian stated plainly.

José shook her head. "Yes, you can. Yes, Gabe loved me, but in that is the implication that he would want me to be happy even without him. Give me a chance. I'll be the best. I promise," José pleaded.

"You really want to go to the dance with someone who blamed you for the death of his friend?" Brian asked.

"But Brian, you stopped blaming me, you said it yourself. That I didn't pull the trigger, Gabe did. Please, Brian," José tried, but it was no use.

"I'm sorry, José. I won't do it. Let me know when you have that looping thing worked out, okay?" Brian walked to the front door. José looked at him with pleading eyes, but all she got in return was cold, emotionless ice. She rushed out the door and drove home crying.

Brian closed the door gently and soon heard José pulling away from the curb. Did he want to go to the dance with her? Of course. She was hot, one hell of a musician and a great person, but he knew the whole time he would be thinking of Gabe, and what he would say if he had stolen José from him. Brian sighed and walked to the kitchen to get a glass of water.

"So what was that all about?" his mom asked, leaning on the countertop.

"Nothing," Brian stated.

"Didn't sound like nothing to me," his mom pushed, "She seems nice. Why not go to the dance with her?"

"Mom, that was the girl Gabe loved. I'm not going to betray him by—"

"She's smart, too. What she said about love it's true. Don't pass her up, hun. Gabe would kick you into next week if he saw you torturing the poor girl like this," his mom finished.

Brian downed the last of his water. Was he torturing her? She clearly wanted to go to the dance with him, and she nearly begged him to go with her. Was he the bad guy? No, he was protecting his friend's memory. Or was he, in a way, betraying it by making José upset? Brian let out a heavy sigh.

"What do you think I should do?" he asked his mother.

"Call her," she said, grabbing the phone, "It's not every day you'll have a girl like that begging you to go on a date."

14

"So, he flat out refused you?" Adrianna asked on the other end of the phone line.

"Yah. I knew he would never ask me because of Gabe, but I figured that if I asked him, he might go for it," José told her friend, practically in tears, lying on her bed. She had no idea why Brian's rejection bothered her so much. She hadn't even cried this hard when her previous boyfriends had dumped her.

"I'm so sorry, sweetie. I know that must have stung," Adrianna said, evidently trying to comfort her friend, "Look at it this way, when one door closes another opens." This made José cry even harder. Was her chance with Brian completely lost? Had she blown it? Before she could answer, she heard her cell phone ring. She picked it up and gasped when she saw the caller ID.

"I have to go," she said into the land line and hung up. She then answered her cell.

"Brian," she stated dryly, desperately trying to hide the fact that she had been crying.

"Look José, I'm so sorry that I made you cry. It was the last thing I wanted. You just caught me off guard, that's all," Brian explained over the phone line.

"Now that you've had time to think it over?" José asked. She saw no reason to beat around the bush, not when she wanted an answer this badly. When she got no response, she pushed on. "I know you're thinking if you go with me that you're going behind Gabe's back, but you were the one who proved to me that I couldn't let that incident control my life. So, name one reason why it should control yours now?"

"You're right. You've never been more right," Brian commented, "I would be honoured to escort you to the dance." José sat straight up in her bed.

"Really?" She asked, not believing what she had heard.

"Yah, it will be fun. I'll have the prettiest date there."

José felt her cheeks blush as her smile grew. "You won't regret this!" After they hung up, José jumped from her bed and threw open her closet, looking for the dress that would most impress Brian.

Brian straightened his suit and knocked on the door. He was happy that he had agreed to go to the dance with José, but he still had that feeling of betraying Gabe. The door opened, and a woman, whom he assumed to be José's mother, invited him inside.

"Thank you, ma'am," Brian replied, stepping inside. "Will José be down shortly?"

"Oh, call me Lidia, sweetie. And she shouldn't be too long," Lidia told Brian, "She's really into this dance." Brian felt his cheeks colour a bit. If only it were the dance she would be interested.

"That's good I guess," Brian stated, playing along. He wanted it to be true. He liked José but wasn't sure if he could have a proper relationship with her.

"You're the boy she's been working on that song with?" Lidia asked. Brian nodded. "Yep, she's really into this dance." With that, they heard footsteps on the staircase. Brian looked up, and his jaw dropped. José was wearing a tight-fitting green sea foam colored dress that became loose at her waist and hung just above her ankles. Her hair had perfect little waves in it and hung loosely, draped over her shoulders, hiding one of the red jewelled earrings that she was wearing. Brian noted the pendant that Gabe had given her around her neck. It sent stabs of guilt threw his gut. As she walked down the stairs, the movement caused the illusion of waves hitting the shore.

"What do you think?" José asked, a hint of nervousness in her voice. Brian was at a loss for words. He opened his mouth, but no words came out. "Well?"

"I can't describe it in words," Brian managed. José smiled, and Brian heard Lidia laugh.

"Now, Brian, take care of my little girl tonight. I want her back here early enough that she isn't a zombie in the morning," Lidia instructed.

"Don't worry," Brian reassured, and with that, they left. He opened the door to his Honda Civic, and José climbed in.

"You look very handsome," José commented as they pulled away from the curb.

"Nothing compared to you," Brian commented, "Not that you're handsome...I mean, you are...But I meant that you're really pretty, not—" Brian stopped as he heard José laugh.

"I knew what you meant," she commented, and then twirled the gold circle of fifths pendant in her fingers. Brian lost his smile. They drove in silence for a few minutes before José spoke again.

"Are you sure you're okay with doing this?"

"Yes," Brian replied hesitantly, "but could you do me a favour?"

"Sure," José replied. Brian chewed his request over in his head, wondering if it was a good idea to ask.

"Never mind," he muttered.

"No, what's the favour?" José pushed, putting a soft hand on Brian's arm. Brian took a deep breath before he spoke again, worried José would get mad at what he was about to ask.

"The pendant. I know you love it and always wear it, but could you take it off tonight? I just don't want that reminder of what I'm doing every time I look at you."

José smiled and kissed him on the cheek, "Sure. But you're not doing anything wrong. Remember that," she said, removing the pendant and placing it in her coat pocket.

Soon, they were pulling into the school parking lot. Brian helped José out of the car, and they walked to the door. Brian's English teacher was the one taking tickets. He smiled as he saw the young couple.

"I'm glad to see you took my advice," Mr. Write commented to Brian, taking the two tickets and marking them off the list.

"Every last word," Brian replied, smiling and placed his hand in José's.

The music was loud in the dance, and the lights flashed and swung around in elaborate patterns around the dance floor. José led Brian over to where her friends were.

"Glad to see you two getting along," Adriana joked, having to yell over the music. She still hadn't fully forgiven Brian for punching out her best friend. "You look super-hot, José."

"You too," José replied, also yelling, and then suddenly pulled Brian closer to her. Brian glanced at her and saw she was staring at something. He followed her line of vision and saw the jock who had punched him in the parking lot. He remembered him saying *"my girl"* and *"she'll come around"*.

"José?" Brian asked. Adriana looked in the direction José was staring and immediately looked at Brian.

"There," she yelled, pointing to the wall, "Now,"

José nodded and took Brian by the hand.

"What's going on?" Brian asked once Adriana had joined them.

"That's Mat Harrison. He is a total jerk and thinks all women are his to do with as he pleases. José is like the only girl from our class he hasn't managed to get into bed. Not for lack of trying, I might add," Adriana explained and got a glare from José.

"*I might add* that he came close because of you!" she snapped. Brian placed a hand on José's shoulder and whispered in her ear.

"Should I be concerned?"

"No," José stated firmly, but Brian could tell she was mad. He led her to the hall where it was quieter.

"Now I'll ask again, should I be concerned for you?"

José looked at Brian, surprised, "What do you mean?"

"Is he going to make you uncomfortable? Is he going to assault you like he did me?" Brian answered. José looked away, only worsening Brian's concern. "What happened?"

"Adriana was drunk, hell, I was drunk. Mat came onto us. Adriana went with him, begging me to go with her, saying it would be fun. I declined. The next day I found out that Mat didn't even give Adriana a good night, he only cared that I declined him. He's been trying to get into my pants ever since," José explained, tears forming in her eyes, "He embarrassed Adriana at school the next day for failing to convince me."

"José, I'm so sorry," Brian said, regretting pushing the subject.

José slipped her arms around him and squeezed him tight. "I know you don't want anything between us, but tonight could you pretend to be mine?" she asked.

Brian was taken aback by this request. He was almost going to argue till he saw José's eyes full of hopeful longing.

"I can do that," Brian stated, squeezing José back.

Then he heard a slow song start to play. He quickly let go of José and raised her hand to his mouth. He kissed it and asked, "Could I have this dance?" He may not want a relationship with José, but after hearing her story, he planned on making this night as special as possible. He led her to the dance floor and held her close as she placed her head on his shoulder. The lighting had changed to a standard blue and white, and green. Squares floated like stars on the ceiling and walls. Brian caught a glance of Adriana, who was smiling and giving him a thumbs up.

After the dance, José and Brian walked slowly to his car. Brian had his arm around José, who was digging through her purse looking for something. When they reached the car, José abruptly turned around and kissed Brian. Brian didn't return the kiss at first, but eventually did.

"Sorry. I needed to do that, at least once," José said calmly and climbed into the black Honda. Brian followed and cranked the heater up to max. He pulled out of the parking lot and glanced at his clock.

"Uhm, Brian, my house is that way," José said as Brian turned towards the park.

"I know. Night's still young, though. Thought a walk under the stars might be nice," Brian responded. José smiled and was soon hanging onto Brian's as if she wished this night would never end. Brian frowned at the thought of having to tell her that he could never be hers.

Patrick Gloutney

José was in absolute heaven. Here under the stars, holding tight to Brian's arm. He had definitely done what she had asked. It really seemed like he was hers. It saddened her that he was only pretending. She had hoped that maybe he would realize he had feelings for her, but she could tell by how stiff he still was with her that it wasn't the case. She had decided to act as though he had her fooled so that she could get the most out of the evening. They took a seat on one of the park benches where José snuggled up against Brian. She could have fallen asleep right there and then if not for the fact that her legs were so cold. The dress she wore was thin, an attempt to stay cool at the excessively warm dance, but now it was a limiting factor to how long she would be able to stay out.

"You getting cold?" Brian asked, running his hand down her leg, evidently feeling the goose bumps on her skin. José nodded, but held Brian still as he tried to move.

"Please don't," she pleaded.

Brian sighed and forced José away. "We're going to freeze if we stay out here," Brian stated.

José frowned but agreed. She was thankful he had made her return to the car as the warmth from the heater washed over her.

"Thank you, Brian," José said, "for a great night. It was nice of you to pretend for me."

Brian was silent for a few minutes before responding, "You know I wasn't completely pretending."

José felt her heart leap. "Really?" she asked.

Brian nodded, "You were really hot tonight. Plus, you're fun to hang out with."

"Do you think you could try?" José asked sheepishly. Brian gave her a look that showed he didn't catch what she meant. "You and I. Do you think we could give a real relationship a try?" Brian was silent again, and José feared breaking it, worrying what his answer was going to be.

"I can't make you stop wearing that pendant," Brian said finally as they turned down José's street.

José nodded, understanding what the response meant. "I would," she ventured, but Brian shook his head. José felt her heart sink. *It was worth a try,* she told herself.

"José I-"

"Don't say it, Brian. I know what you're going to say, and I don't want to hear it." José interrupted as they pulled into her laneway. Brian reached out for her arm but José pulled away, not wanting to get hurt anymore, not after such a perfect evening.

"Thank you for a great night," she said, the remorse clear in her voice, and climbed out of the car. Brian grabbed her by the shoulder as she reached her door. He turned her around and kissed her. José let her purse fall from her hands, completely caught off guard. Brian broke the kiss and staggered backwards.

"You didn't let me finish," he panted, "I want to give us a try," José swore her heart was about to jump out of her mouth.

"You do?" she questioned, not believing what she had heard.

"Yes. What you've said has been right, all of it. Gabe would kill me if I passed up an opportunity like this, particularly if he saw how happy it would make you. I can't possibly betray him, because this is what he would want," Brian explained.

José smiled bigger than she even thought possible. She threw her arms around Brian. "Thank you," she said happily.

"Now go in and get some rest. I don't want to get on your mom's bad side," Brian said, kissing her forehead.

José nodded. She waved goodbye as Brian pulled away. She then walked into the house and let out a scream. Her mother came running down the stairs.

"José? Are you alright?" she asked, concern filled her voice. José straightened her dress before responding.

"I, have never been better."

Patrick Gloutney

José practically floated down the halls, so light on her feet that she was almost skipping. She had been smiling since she got home last night, and now was no exception. When she got to her locker, Adriana was waiting for her.

"Someone's happy today," Adriana commented, as José quickly opened her lock. "So, how'd it go with you and Brian after the dance?"

"It was good," José said, trying not to give the whole evening away.

"I'd say it went better than just well. I haven't seen you this happy in a long time," Adriana pushed. José laughed. It felt good to be happy again.

"Well, we went for a walk in the park—,"

"How romantic," Adriana interrupted.

"Then when we got home, he kissed me goodnight," José finished. She saw her friend smile.

"So, are you and him, you know, you and him?" José nodded. "Oh, José, I'm so happy it worked out."

"I am too. I really didn't think it would." José stated, closing her locker.

"So did you two...take it upstairs?" José playfully hit her friend's shoulder.

"Of course not! You know I'm not that kind of girl."

"I had to ask. Let me guess, you're not going to be in the cafeteria today, right?"

"Correct. Brian and I are going to work on the song," José responded as they walked to homeroom.

"You have to let me sit in one of these days," Adriana said. José considered it but decided against it.

"You'll hear it at the concert like everyone else." Adriana shook her head.

"You and your music. I still can't believe all this drama came from one nerd." José stopped dead in her tracks. Adriana looked back at her, puzzled. José twirled the pendant around her neck between her fingers, suddenly feeling guilty for promising Brian, she wouldn't wear it.

"You, okay?" Adriana asked.

"Please don't call Gabe a nerd," José stated sternly.

José undid the clasp on her pendant's chain and slipped it into her purse before entering the music room. She had promised Brian she would stop wearing it, but it still didn't feel right to her. So, she had reached the conclusion she wouldn't wear it when she was with Brian. José wasn't surprised to find Brian was already practicing his part when she walked in. She placed her stuff on a chair and walked to the practice room Brian was occupying, grabbing a school guitar on the way.

"Hey," she said, opening the door.

"Hey, back," Brian replied. José leaned over the drum kit and gave him a quick kiss on the cheek.

"So, I wrote a guitar part the other day that I think will fit really nicely..." The two musicians worked on their song for the better part of the lunch hour before deciding that they needed to eat something before their afternoon classes.

José had just placed the piece of carrot impaled on her fork in her mouth when she noticed Brian looking at her chest. She looked down to see if she had anything on her shirt. Much to her displeasure, there was nothing.

So much for him being different, she thought to herself. Most of the guys José had been with only wanted her for her body. José had thought, and hoped, Brian would be different. Apparently, she had thought wrong.

"See something you like," José remarked drily. Her statement seemed to startle Brian.

"No! Well...yes...but not the way you're thinking...not that I wouldn't—" He stammered. José waved a dismissive hand.

"Save it," she muttered in disappointment.

"I wasn't looking for that reason!" Brian snapped. "I saw you earlier today with Adriana. You had your pendant on, but you don't have it on now," he finished, his tone softening. The food José was swallowing caught in her throat, causing her to cough. She had hoped he wouldn't see her with it on, but she realized now that was almost an impossibility.

"Sorry. Force of habit. I didn't even realize I had it on till the second period," she lied. There were a few moments of silence before Brian responded.

"José, listen, it was selfish of me to ask you to stop wearing that pendant. I know how much it means to you and why you wear it." José glanced at her purse, not sure where this was going. "I don't want you to change for me. If you did, then you wouldn't be you, would you?" Now José was completely lost. Every guy she had been with had wanted her to change in some way. From asking her not to talk about music so much, all the way up to asking her to wear skimpier outfits and act as though she was their property. That José particularly hated, the notion that she could belong to someone. She noticed Brian was waiting for a response, but had none, not a word. She was completely caught off guard.

"I don't know what to say," she managed.

"Here," Brian stated and grabbed the chain that José hadn't fully tucked into her purse. He then moved behind her, and she felt the cold metal brush against her collarbone as he reattached the clasp.

"I'm sorry I ever asked you to stop wearing it," Brian whispered in her ear, then placed a soft kiss on her neck before returning to his lunch. José melted right there. She wanted to say something sweet, something that would tell Brian how perfect he seemed to her at that exact moment. What she said made her scold herself more severely than she thought possible.

"I don't understand." José immediately buried her face in her hands, her face burning red in embarrassment. Did she really just say that? Was she that pathetic? To her relief, she heard Brian laugh. She lifted her head and managed a small laugh.

"I thought you had a boyfriend before," Brian joked. It made José smile when he referred to himself as her boyfriend.

"I can't believe I just said that," José muttered.

"Maybe we should stop by the library and take out a book for you."

José playfully punched Brian in the arm.

"I know damn well what I'm doing when it comes to relationships," José stated firmly, "I've never been with someone who knows how to make a girl feel special."

Patrick Gloutney

"Could you pass me that wrench on the table?" Brian asked from under his Honda Civic. He felt it tap against his knee a few moments later. He took it and tightened the oil drain plug on his engine.

"Why don't you just bring your car to a garage like everyone else?" José asked as he slid out from under his car.

"I don't believe in paying someone to do something I can do on my own," Brian replied simply and popped his hood.

"Seems like a big mess to save a few bucks," José retorted.

"I enjoy doing it." While Brian was pouring the new oil into his engine, he felt a hand run up his back. He and José were in his parents' garage. She had called, wondering what he was up to. He told her and expected her to just brush it off and do something with her friends; instead, she showed up at his door ten minutes later. He felt completely underdressed. José was wearing stylish tight tight-fitting blue jeans, elegant black heeled winter boots and a flannel shirt that was cut to hug her body just right. Brian was wearing a pair of oil-covered sweat pants and a baggy T-shirt.

"How often are you supposed to change the oil in a car anyway?" José asked, pulling Brian from his thoughts.

"Depends. I do it when I see it needs doing. But I'd say rule of thumb...every six months at least," Brian answered, wiping down the dip stick.

"So, if my mom's car needed an oil change, you'd do it for me?" José asked, leaning on him as if trying to be cute.

Brian laughed. "Yah. I could lend you my car for a day and take your mom's car home with me," He was puzzled when this idea seemed to surprise José.

"You'd let me drive your car?" she asked.

Brian shrugged. "Why not. You've probably been driving as long me, and your mom's car doesn't look like it has any dents in it," Brian reasoned, still wondering why José was surprised. "You could bring it over and wait for it like today, but I figured you'd rather not."

"I don't know. I think it's pretty cool how you can do this stuff," José stated, and then pressed herself against Brian, forcing him to brace himself against his car, kissing him on the nose. "I enjoyed myself today."

Brian smiled. There was definitely something different with José. All the girls he knew wouldn't touch him after working on a car; they wouldn't even have been in the same room as the oil now sitting in a container on the workbench.

"I'll pull your car in and do a check before you go," Brian said, and closed his hood. He started his engine, gunned it a few times to try and get a laugh or smile out of José, and it worked. He then climbed into her car and pulled it into the garage. He set to work checking all the fluids. The oil was fine, must have been changed recently. The only thing low was the brake fluid, but Brian just assumed that the car needed a brake job.

"Hey José, could you pass me the tire iron in that corner?" He waited for the tool, but it didn't come. He looked to see José looking at something on the workbench. He walked up behind and sighed when he saw what she was looking at.

"Sorry, I meant to deal with those before you saw them." José gave him a look that demanded an explanation. "It's not what it looks like."

"What does it look like?" she asked. Brian pointed to a box on the edge of the workbench.

"They were from Gabe's room. He used to find photos of you on the school sites and social networking sites and make these," Brian explained. "These were my favourites."

"They're beautiful," José remarked. Brian looked at her, surprised at her acceptance of the photos.

"Really? Most people would consider it stalking."

"I think it's flattering," José answered, "Particularly this one." She held up a photo of herself outside at a school event, only Gabe had tinted it black and white so that it looked like the light was only on her, and then he had surrounded the edge of the picture with a snowflake-type pattern. It had been Gabe's favourite. Brian remembered the day Gabe had shown it to him, full of pride at the fact that he could make his dream girl look even more desirable. Brian scanned the other photos José had pulled out and felt his eye widen when he saw one that had red lines running sporadically threw it.

"So why didn't Gabe's parent keep..." José stopped as Brian grabbed the picture that had caught his eye. He stuffed it into his pocket. "What was that?"

"Nothing. Gabe's parents didn't want them; it reminded them too much of—"

"Brian, what are you hiding?" José pushed, then her eyes widened, "It's not like a nude pic or anything, is it?"

"No. Geez, Gabe would never do something like that," Brian quickly responded, defending his friend.

"Brian," José stated in her forceful tone. She had a look in her eye that almost screamed danger to Brian.

"It's nothing important," Brian replied, his tone equally forceful. Then José quickly reached out and snatched the picture that was partially sticking out of his pocket. She opened it before Brian could protest.

"Oh, this one is nice," José stated, "What are the red lines? They seem out of place." Brian sighed heavily. He wasn't sure he should tell her about that picture; it might send her screaming. He gently took the picture from her and set it down on the table.

"Brian? What's wrong?"

"That was the picture that Gabe had in front of him when I found him. The lines are where the blood seeped through the cracked glass."

José frantically rubbed soap over her hands, rinsing them again, but she still felt as though she had blood on her hands, even though she knew it was ridiculous. The blood would have been dry after all. She should have listened to Brian and just left it at "not important". It was important, though, otherwise Brian wouldn't have kept it. José looked up at her reflection in the mirror and saw that her makeup had begun to run. She hadn't cried since she started going out with Brian. She sighed heavily.

How could he let me hold that thing so freely? She asked herself. *You idiot, you're the one who stole it from his pocket.* José sighed again, regretting ignoring Brian's warnings and began to clean herself up. She opened the cabinet, hoping Brian's mother had a cloth or something hidden in there. What she saw made her heart sink. On the bottom shelf was a prescription bottle with Brian's name on it. She grabbed it to make sure she had read it right. She had; they were antidepressants. Fear welled up inside her. That's when a knock came at the door.

"José, are you okay?" Brian asked.

José forgot about her makeup; she opened the door and hugged Brian tightly. "Don't leave me," she murmured. She was scared more than she thought possible. She knew Gabe had been depressed, and she didn't want Brian following the same path.

"What?" he asked, pulling away from her to look her in the eye. He then seemed to notice the pill bottle in José's hand. "Oh."

"Why didn't you tell me?" José asked, tears forming in her eyes.

"Well, first off, my problems are my problems—"

"Wrong. They're our problems!" José snapped, "You can tell me anything. I want to help. Lord knows you've helped me." Brian raised an eyebrow. José knew she had a tear rolling down her face, and that her grip on the pill bottle was weakening. She had never been so afraid of losing anyone before. "Just promise me you won't make the same mistake Gabe did."

"I promise," Brian quickly replied.

José smiled and wrapped her arms around him once again. "I can't bear to lose you," she whispered. "I love you." José immediately felt a shift in Brian; he tensed up, and he let his arms fall to his sides. José bit her lower lip, praying she hadn't made a mistake. She had never truly meant those words to anyone, except now, and she hoped she hadn't just scared Brian away.

Brian pulled away from the embrace and pulled an oil-covered rag from his pocket and wiped it across his forehead, leaving a blackish trail behind it. "Your mom's car is all ready to go. Nothing major. It might need a brake job soon though."

José nodded her thanks and rushed out to the car. She pulled down the road but had to pull over as she started to cry again. Had she just blown it with Brian?

You stupid idiot, she thought to herself. The feeling of loss was too much for her to bear, and she could barely keep her eyes open as she fumbled with her cellphone. She managed to dial her home number after a few failed attempts.

"Mom," she sobbed, "I need you to come and get...I can't drive like this."

Patrick Gloutney

Brian sat at the island in his kitchen, staring at the glass of water in his hand, when his mom opened the door.

"Hey sweetie, how was your day?" she asked, placing some bags on the counter.

"Got the oil changed in my car. Did a check on José's as well," Brian responded, taking a big sip from his water.

"I'm sure she appreciated that," his mother replied absent-mindedly, unpacking the bags, "I was thinking Mexican tonight."

"Sure, whatever," Brian said. His mother looked at him and put what she was carrying on the table.

"What's wrong?" she asked.

Brian shook his head, "Nothing."

"I know you better than that. You love Mexican. Trouble with José?" his mother asked.

Brian smiled a little. His mother seemed to have a way of reading him like a book. He always knew he could approach her with anything. She was the one he approached when he suspected he had depression. She had taken him to see someone about it the next day and was always supportive of him through it all.

"She saw those pictures I got from Gabe's house."

His mother raised an eyebrow. "So? They're all very flattering."

"That's not what the problem was. When she saw the picture with the blood on it she freaked and went to wash her hands and found my antidepressant meds. I guess it scared her somehow, and she told me she loved me." Brian explained.

"Oh, honey. That's normally a good thing."

Brian downed the last of his water, "I didn't say it back."

His mother nodded and placed her "What did you say?"

"I told her all was well with her mom's car, and then she left," he responded. His mom nodded.

"Why didn't you say it back?"

"Because I'm an idiot," Brian responded.

"Do you love her?"

"I don't know. I really like her, but I don't know what love is supposed to feel like."

His mom let out a short laugh. "Honey, no one ever does." She started to put the perishables away as she continued, "Let me ask you this. Can you stand the idea of losing her? You don't have to tell me, but if the thought upsets you, then you might want to do something about it."

Brian considered his mother's words. He remembered the way José had been when she found his medication. How much of a wreck she was, fearing that he would take his own life. The more he thought about it, the more the thought of losing José upset him. The more he wanted her.

Brian stood up from his chair, "Thanks, mom. You just made things really clear,"

"Anytime."

Patrick Gloutney

José sat on her bed, trying to focus on the magazine she had in her hands, but she couldn't fight back the tears. How could three little words make such a mess of everything? It made no sense. She heard a knock on her door and jumped.

"José? Sweetie? Are you alright?" her mother asked. José didn't answer. She wanted to be left alone, to wallow in her sorrow. Of course, her mother wouldn't have that and opened the door. "What happened at Brian's today?"

"I screwed up, mom," José sobbed, "I screw up bad, really bad."

"Oh, come on, I doubt it could be that bad. What did you do, hit Brian for being a little too quick?" her mother asked, rubbing her hand up and down José's back.

"God no. Brian wouldn't do anything unless I started it," José responded, wiping yet another tear from her eye.

"Then what happened?"

"He's on antidepressants," José muttered.

"So?" her mother pushed.

"Gabe had depression," José answered.

Her mother sighed. "Sweetie, you need to trust that Brian won't do anything. If he's on medication, then it means he's getting help. The best thing you can do is support him, but that's not what's upsetting you, is it?"

"I told him I loved him," José said softly, "He didn't say it back."

There was a long moment of silence before José's mother spoke again. "You probably just surprised him."

"You think so?" José asked.

"Yeah, I think so. Was he flustered afterwards?"

"He wiped his forehead with an oily rag," José lamented.

Her mother laughed. "Men can be idiots when caught off guard."

"Why wouldn't he say something then? Like, thank you or something?" José asked.

"Okay, even I know that sounds lame," her mother stated, smiling, "He probably didn't know what to say."

José considered the thought and found it made sense. Then she heard her phone ding. She quickly grabbed it and saw the text was from Brian. She read it and let out a sigh of relief mixed with anxiety. He wanted to meet with her in the park.

Her mother read the text over José's shoulder. "See. You didn't screw up at all."

José hugged her mom. "Thanks, Mom. Want to help pick something out that will sweep him off his feet?" José asked.

"I would love to, not that you'll need it."

José climbed out of her car and took a deep breath of the cold air. She was wearing a burgundy wool hat, a matching stylish winter coat that ended just below her knees and, under that was a simple set of bootcut jeans and a white blouse. She had originally thought to overdress to try and impress Brian, but was glad that she had decided against it. She also wore very little makeup, with only a hint of eyeliner.

Brian's text said to meet in the park, but not where in the park. José didn't see his Honda anywhere, so she decided to walk the trail and wait for him. The town had put up Christmas lights since the dance, and it was starting to snow lightly. It made her think of the black and white photo she had been looking at in Brian's garage, wondering whatever possessed Gabe to do such a thing, and what devotion he would have had towards her. It made guilt swirl inside her to think that she hadn't even noticed him for the past few years, and that she had been so naïve to think she would have ever been able to make it up to him if he hadn't killed himself.

Why didn't he ever say something to me? She wondered, but she knew the answer. She was popular, not the prettiest, but still pretty enough, and hung around with the girls who wouldn't even consider associating with Gabe unless absolutely necessary. To someone of Gabe's social status, José was unapproachable. It was a thought that disgusted José even more every time it crossed her mind. She scanned the parking lot looking for Brian's car as she completed the lap around the park, but she didn't see it. She sighed heavily and pulled her phone from her pocket, wondering if there was more information from Brian. There wasn't.

Where the hell is he? She asked herself. That's when she noticed the lights on her car were on. She walked over and noticed a picture lying on the passenger seat. Puzzled, she grabbed it. It was a picture of Brian and Gabe leaning on a red sports car. She recognized it instantly. It was the car that she had seen when she went to see Gabe's parents. She looked around and saw it sitting at the far end of the parking lot. She locked her car and hurried over. When she saw who was sitting inside, she froze. It was Gabe's father. José jumped when the door opened. What was he doing here? She was supposed to meet Brian. Had he set her up? Gabe's father climbed out of his car and walked towards José. She wasn't sure if she wanted to stay or run to her car and drive home to hide in her room.

"José?" the man asked. José nodded slowly, feeling a little betrayed by Brian. "Don't be mad at Brian. He had the full intention of meeting you here today. He'll be by later. I made him let me talk with you first."

"How did you get into my car?" José asked, more bluntly than she had meant to.

"Old habits die hard. I was arrested at 21 for grand theft auto. I've cleaned up since then, but I still know the tricks," Gabe's father explained. José was surprised. From the little she knew of the man, she had thought of him as a reputable businessman, not a car thief. Then again, everyone had a past.

"I am truly sorry for every part I had in your son's death," José said softly, hoping he would finally accept her apology.

The man nodded. "I want you to stop seeing Brian."

José looked at him, surprised. "What?"

"Brian's a good kid. I'm worried you'll corrupt him," Gabe's father explained.

"I'm not corrupting Brian. We've helped each other through this mess," José argued.

"Brian forgave you for my son's death. He convinced my wife to do the same. He nearly tricked me as well. But I saw through the game you were playing. You just want the blame to fall elsewhere."

"I really don't think it's your place to decide who Brian can date. That's up to his parents if anything, certainly not you," José stated coldly.

"Brian is like a son to me. You took one from me. I won't let you take the other," Gabe's father shouted. José noticed a passerby looking towards them. She thought she knew him, but couldn't place him.

"I am sure that Brian can make his own decisions. I will not stop seeing him. He's the best thing that I have ever found, and you've got another thing coming if you think I will let him go so easily," José yelled back and turned to her car.

Gabe's father grabbed her arm, spinning her back around. "You'll watch your mouth, young lady!" José heard a car drive into the parking lot, its headlights flood over her and Gabe's father.

"Jake!" Brian yelled, "Let her go." Jake looked up, seemingly surprised at Brian's presence. He looked at his watch.

"You said thirty minutes," he commented.

"I changed my mind," Brian stated forcefully, "She's not the reason Gabe pulled that damn trigger. No one made him do that. He did it himself, and we have no right to lay blame."

Jake waved a dismissive hand, "You can't possibly say you have no anger towards her. She pulled that prank. Her picture was in front of him! How could you date your best friend's girl?"

"How could you assault your son's dream girl?" Brian shot back.

José remained silent, stunned. How could he defend her like this? Jake and he were closer than she and Brian were, yet he stood up for her. Surely some of what Jake said was true. Surely Brian still harboured some resentment towards her part in Gabe's death. The fact that he kept defending her only reinforced the feelings she had for him.

"You've changed," Jake spat.

"Only for the better," Brian responded, pulling José close to him, "I think you'd better go."

Jake muttered something inaudible and slammed the door of his sports car. He pulled away, tires spinning and sending a spray of snow at them.

José looked at Brian shell shocked. "Thank you." She pulled away, not sure where they stood.

"Let's walk," Brian suggested, and José eagerly nodded, ignoring the fact that her hands and feet were beginning to freeze. They walked in silence for a while before she gathered the courage to speak.

"I'm sorry, Brian," she said.

"For?"

"The 'I love you' thing. I shouldn't have said it," José replied.

"Did you mean it?" Brian asked.

José gave him a look. "Of course. But I should have waited a little longer, I guess."

Brian shook his head. "You just startled me, that's all. No one has ever said it the way you said it to me."

José smiled. "So, we're good?" Brian nodded. José kissed him and rested her head on his shoulder. She felt all the tensions of the day just melt away. She could have stayed like that the whole night, resting against Brian, the Christmas lights all around the snow-covered park with big fat snowflakes falling all around them.

"You're shivering," Brian commented.

"I'm a little cold," José admitted.

"Here, let's go to my car. I'll crank up the heater and then I'll take you for dinner."

José's smile broadened, "That would be wonderful."

Patrick Gloutney

Brian sucked back the last of his drink and leaned back in the plastic McDonald's chair. He looked over at José who was enjoying a salad. She may not have been the prettiest girl in school by anyone else's standards, but with the minuscule amount of makeup and the simple outfit she had on, no one came close to Brian. He was glad that he hadn't let their relationship fall apart over something as stupid as a few words.

"I should take you out more often. You're a cheap date," Brian commented.

José laughed. "My mother accuses me of not eating enough to keep a bird alive. Besides I have a boyfriend I need to watch my figure for." Brian smiled as they both laughed.

"Maybe I should start working out then," Brian joked.

"I have one question. How did you know to come early?" José asked after swallowing another mouthful of lettuce.

"A friend saw you. He gave me a call and said you looked scared. I was waiting a few blocks away, so it didn't take long," Brian responded, wiping his mouth with his napkin.

"Remind me to give that friend a kiss," José commented playfully. Brian nodded and stayed quiet, content to watch José as she finished her salad. He noted that she had the circle of fifths pendant on and was glad. He wanted her, just the way she was. He didn't want her to change in any way. Even if it meant him changing to accommodate her.

After they finished their meal, the young couple walked back hand-in-hand to the park, content in each other's presence.

When they got to José's mother's car, she climbed in and started up the engine, then climbed back out as she waited for it to warm up. "Why not drive here?"

"And miss a chance to walk down moonlit streets with you? I'd rather bear the cold back to my car a hundred times over before passing that up," Brian responded.

José smiled and wrapped her arms around him in a loving embrace. "That's so sweet." The two of them stayed still, silent. Brian didn't want the moment to end, but the inevitable was unfortunately close. He leaned his head down to José and kissed her.

"I love you," he said softly.

He felt José smile against his kiss. "I love you too,"

With that, Brian let her go and helped her into her car. "You ready for that show next week?"

"Don't worry, we're going to do fine," José reassured. Brian didn't respond. He was nervous about the whole thing. As it was, he had never thought his singing voice was very good, but José seemed to think it was all right. The thought of standing up in front of all the people he had known for so long, and doing something that he would normally never do, scared him, although he'd never admit it.

He felt José's hand grasp his arm. "I meant it,"

Brian smiled and nodded. "I know. So tomorrow, bring your mom's car over and I'll get the parts for the brake job."

Patrick Gloutney

There were a few claps across the gym as the last act finished. The act had been okay; it was a bunch of guys acting crazy, doing an air band rock-and-roll version of Carol of the Bells. The Tech Team had really been the ones that saved them, with random lighting patterns distracting the audience from the horrible synchronization of the boys on stage. Brian swallowed hard. He had never remembered ever being so nervous in his life. He was wearing dress pants and a white dress shirt. José stood next to him in an elegant black dress, her hair pinned up just right, and her makeup was shaded to accent her eyes and cheekbones.

She looked at him and must have seen how nervous he was. "Hey, it's going to be okay. You're going to knock them dead,"

Brian nodded nervously. Not only was he going to do this, but he was starting the whole thing off. He felt the knot in his stomach grow even bigger as the Master of Ceremonies desperately tried to get the interest of the crowd back.

"Now we have a special treat. Two of our students have put together a little song for us using different..." the speaker stopped to read the card he was holding "layers of music. Let's hear it for them." There was one clap from the whole audience of 500 students, who were all required to be there. Brian never understood why they forced the students to attend, but he figured it was a control issue.

José took his hand and led him up onto the stage. His heartbeat was deafening in his ears as the lights spun onto him and José as they took their seats. José was moving so smoothly, as if she had no stage fright at all, but a glance she gave Brian showed she was also a little nervous, not that the audience would ever be able to tell. She took her microphone and nodded to Brian.

"Hi everyone. I know you don't really want to be here, so I'll keep this short. We would like to dedicate this song to Gabe Ledford. I didn't know him personally. I'm sure most of you heard of the prank I pulled on him a while back..." This resulted in a round of short chuckles from the crowd. "Well, that was wrong of me," José stated firmly, reaching up to twirl the pendant she had from Gabe between her fingers. "I hope you all know that. I put him, his family, his friends, and most of all Brian through hell and back. So could you please all remember Gabe with this song, and remember not to make the same mistakes I did?"

José replaced the microphone, and Brian could see a small tear run down the side of her face. He felt some welling in his eyes as well at the thought of his friend. Images of the day he had found him flashed through his mind, and all the old feelings rushed in.

He nodded to José and hit the kick drum pedal. José pressed the first pedal on the looping board, and a soft guitar part began to play from the speakers. Brian rolled on the snare drum and then started his hitting pattern as José began to play her part. Brian waited the right amount of time and leaned into the microphone.

"He was like a brother to me,
Like a member of the family
Stayin' over on Friday Nights," he sang. José chimed in with her backup part.

"Every time I look at you now,
All I see is you blaming yourself
On the day his world came crashin' down, Brian slammed the kick drum and changed his snare pattern as José came in

"That boy,
He had a beautiful heart that I shattered like glass," José sang
"That boy's still in love with you."
"If I could, I'd erase every teardrop stain I left on his face,
Sometimes I wish I had never knew...that boy"

Brian felt a tear run down the side of his face as José played her piano solo.

"I see the guilt fill up your eyes,
Every time you apologize,
"'Cause your story is still full of blame," Brian continued when she was done. With that, the flood lights snapped on and the spotlights moved to show spinning stars dancing across the walls in elaborate patterns. Brian made a note to thank the Tech Team for their efforts.

"Gotta know where I'm comin' from
I was the bullet out of his gun

What I did can't be undone," José sang, the regret in his voice clear.
"I'd do anything for..."
"That boy,
He had a beautiful heart that I shattered like glass."
"That boy's still in love with you."

That's where Brian's drum solo came in. He ran his sticks across the drum kit and gave it his all. Playing everything with as much precision as possible, nailing it better than ever before and then singing with more expression than he thought he had.

"Every day livin' drowning in your regrets
They may forgive, but you won't forget,
What you did to...that boy, he had a beautiful heart you didn't shatter like glass,"
"That boy is dead because of me."
"If I could, I'd erase every teardrop stain he left on your face,
Sometimes I wish you never knew...that boy,"
"That boy..." José sang mournfully and slowly began to fade the music out. Then Brian thought of something they hadn't practiced but would fit.

"...never faulted you," he finished, just as the music died off.

The crowd was silent as the moving lights returned to focus on the two young performers, and the flood lights dimmed off. Brian felt his nerves returning. Did they not like it? Did it even matter? He had done right by his friend. Even so, he still wanted some form of response, if not for any other reason than to end the tension in the air. There were a couple of claps that came from the silence, then a few more. Applause soon ran through the gym like wildfire, and people began standing up. Before long, the whole student body and teachers were giving Brian and José a standing ovation. Brian smiled, the tension in his body melting away as he glanced at José, who took his hand during their bow. The Tech Team put a slowly spinning star around them as they came back up. Then the crowd did something completely unexpected.

"Kiss! Kiss! Kiss!" they all began shouting. Brian looked at José, it was evident that she was thinking the same thing he was. Leave it to the students to completely throw the meaning of the song out the window.

Brian gave José a gentle hug before taking the microphone. Before he could speak, a projector beeped, and the crowd fell silent. Brian looked to the Tech Team. One was pointing to the wall next to him. Brian looked to see an image of him and Gabe in the school field during the Relay for Life event a few years ago. They were smiling, dressed in neon colours along with the rest of their Relay team, who were playing a game behind them. Underneath the image were the words:

In memory of Gabe Ledford. Let his legacy be a reminder to all of the impact of their actions.

Brian replaced the microphone on its stand; there was nothing more to say. He took José's hand and led her off the stage.

Patrick Gloutney

27

José skipped down the stair's backstage. She spun on her heels and hugged Brian and kissing him.

"I can't believe it!" she shrieked, "That went so well. And the Tech Team...wow! Where did they even get that picture?" Brian smiled. It had gone perfectly, and José was right, the dedication the Tech Team had made ended it beautifully. He was now even farther indebted to them.

He wiped a streak of smeared makeup away from José's face. "You got quite emotional out there."

José placed a playful tap on his shoulder. "I saw you crying too, you know." They both turned to the sound of clapping.

"Well done, both of you," Mr. Wright said, smiling.

"I'd say," the music teacher said from beside Brian's English teacher, "I knew José had talent, but Brian...you have to take music next semester."

"Told you you'd be fantastic," José stated.

"Now, the two of you, get out there. You were the second last act, and that means they are going to announce the winning act," Mr. Write said with a wink. José and Brian walked out just as the music started playing. The image of Gabe and Brian is still projected on the wall.

"Now I'm sure everyone knows who the winner of this year's talent show is. Drum roll, please..." the Master of Ceremonies stated. A drum roll echoed through the gym, and the moving spotlight went to the ceiling. "...That Boy by Brian and José!" The spots quickly swung to the young couple in the corner of the gym. A round of applause went through the gym. José snuggled up against Brian as the M.C. dismissed the students. He and José got many compliments from various students as they made their way out of the gym, eager for the two weeks off ahead of them.

"That was amazing, guys," Adriana complimented, catching up with them, "I'm jealous, José. Your boyfriend is cute and talented."

José laughed and hugged her friend, "Thanks, Adriana. What did you want to do again, Brian?"

"You owe someone a kiss," he stated simply.

José looked at him, puzzled. "I do?"

Brian nodded and led José to the Tech Team desk, where they were packing up. He grabbed one of the cables and began wrapping it the way Gabe had shown him. Although Gabe had never officially been part of the school's Tech Team, he still helped out when he could, picking up some of the basic tricks and passing them on to Brian. "Hey guys, thanks for the light show."

"You kidding? That was fun. There was nothing else we could have been that creative with," the Student Coordinator, Adam, replied.

"I really need to thank you for the picture," Brian stated, pointing to the wall.

"It was a bit of a rush to get it up, but it was worth it," Adam replied, "I could see you guys didn't think the whole kiss thing was appropriate."

Brian looked at José. She seemed perplexed. "Adam, this is José."

"She needs no introduction," Adam commented. Shaking her outstretched hand.

"I'm sorry, but where have I seen you before?"

"Oh, I doubt you saw me. But everyone knows you, particularly now," Adam stated.

Brian saw a glint of recognition pass through José's eyes as she understood why Brian had brought her over. "You were the guy who called Brian the other night."

Adam nodded sheepishly. "You looked like you needed help." José smiled and gave Adam a kiss on the lips.

Adam staggered backwards. "Thank you. I certainly did," José stated nonchalantly, like she hadn't just made the poor kid's week.

Brian laughed.

"You're...you're welcome," Adam managed. The other members of the team were staring at them, seemingly shocked.

"We'll let you get back to work, thanks again for everything," José suggested and pulled Brian out into the hall.

"That was nice of you," Brian said as they entered the now quiet south wing of the school. Being the last day of school before the holidays, no one was sticking around long. "Just don't make a habit of it."

José laughed brightly. "Wouldn't dream of it."

Patrick Gloutney

Brian laughed when his little sister let out a scream as she opened her gift. Her pigtails bounced all around as she ran to give his mother and father a hug, thanking them for her new toy. Brian envied her in some way. She was only six, no real responsibilities, no job, no drama in her life, none that lasted anyway. Most of all, she had never truly experienced loss. She had never known Gabe really all that well, so it was easy for Brian and his parents to protect her after his death. Brian had agreed one hundred percent with his parents' decisions. There was no reason for her to have to go through what Brian had.

"I'll be right back," Brian told his mother, who nodded. They had been unwrapping gifts all morning, and Brian was glad that his sister's was the last one. He walked to the bathroom, closed the door and took the bottle containing his antidepressants. He paused before taking them, wondering if he needed them. He had been pretty happy all morning. Heck, he had been happy all break leading up to today. He and José had spent as much time as possible together; José had even come to start working at the diner where Brian worked as a delivery man. He opened his phone and looked at the picture of José on the lock screen.

He sighed and took the medication. *Better do what the doctor said.* As he walked out back towards the living room, he heard his little sister say.

"Who's that, mommy?" Brian moved to draw back the curtain to see what his sister was looking at. It was José standing on the step about to ring the doorbell. "I'll get it," his sister said before Brian could react.

"Tara, wait," Brian protested, but his sister was already at the door.

"Wow," Tara said, staring at José, "Are you a Christmas fairy?"

Brian heard José laugh at the comment. "Why, thank you, but no, unfortunately, I'm not. However, this might help you find one," José handed Tara a wrapped rectangle. Tara opened it, and her eyes grew to the size of as saucers she opened it.

"Wow! Finding the Hidden Fairies," she exclaimed. Brian walked up with his mother to the door. "Look, mommy!"

"Why don't you go ask for daddy's help with that sweetie?" Brian's mother suggested. Tara nodded eagerly and ran off with her new book.

"I hope she's into that kind of stuff," José remarked. This got a laugh out of both Brian and his mother.

"You have no idea. Merry Christmas, hon," Brian's mother replied, shaking her head while slightly rolling her eyes. "You'll stay for brunch?"

José shook her head, "I've eaten already. I was wondering if I could borrow Brian."

"Sure thing. You two behave," Brian's mother said and walked to the kitchen.

"Grab your coat. Where going for a walk?" José instructed, and Brian willingly complied.

"So how was your Christmas morning?" he asked as they walked down the street.

"Not bad. I love your gift," José said, pushing hair back to display the earrings she had on. "Pretty clever asking my mom to put them under the tree for you. Sorry, I didn't have anything to put under yours."

"Don't worry about it," Brian replied. He hadn't even missed the gift anyway. He hadn't expected or wanted anything from her.

"It was too big to wrap," José said, and the lights on one of the cars parked along the street flashed. Brian raised an eyebrow at her. She pulled a set of keys out of her pocket and handed them to Brian.

"Found it sitting behind my grandfather's garage. When I told him who it was for, he was more than happy to let me take it," she explained.

Brian's jaw dropped as they neared the car. It was a 1980 electric blue Camaro with two black racing stripes running along the hood and roof. "I don't believe this."

"I had him put in a keyless entry system," José commented.

"I don't know what to say, José, this is amazing."

"Don't thank me yet. It's a fixer-upper. My grandfather said something about its engine being tired. He started explaining something about piston rings, and I zoned out, but I thought that you'd be able to figure it out. I'll give you his number if you want to talk with him." José said flatly, then pushed herself against Brian, who, by now, had popped the hood and was looking at the engine underneath it. "I was thinking we could work on it together."

Brian looked at her. "You want to fix a car?"

"You can do it, why can't I?" José replied.

"You know you'll probably get covered in oil at some point," Brian said, skeptical that José would put up with that.

"I'll get used to it."

"How did I get so lucky?" Brian asked.

"You didn't let social status determine who your friends are," José answer, "Now why don't we take this bad boy for a spin?" Brian nodded eagerly and shut the hood. Once inside he turned the key. The engine came alive with a roar. Brian held down the clutch and gunned the engine a few times. He immediately discovered what José's grandfather had meant. The engine was definitely tired, but not dead.

"You'll have to teach me to drive a standard," José remarked.

Brian gave her a look. "How did you get the car here if you can't drive it?"

José smiled, "My mom," she leaned over and kissed him "Merry Christmas babe. Now show me what this thing can do." Brian easily complied. He gunned the engine one more time and then slipped it into gear, speeding away from the curb.

Acknowledgments

I would like to acknowledge the contributions of Sharyn Heagle, who provided moral and technical support, along with knowledge to which I would not otherwise have had access. Without her, this book would not have been possible. Thanks to my family and friends who stood behind me and put up with the process of my writing this manuscript. Thanks to you all.

A special thanks to Craig Sheridan, who was always there and willing to help.

Born in Nova Scotia, Patrick Gloutney always held an interest in storytelling: Putting pen to paper at a relatively young age. After moving to Ottawa, and interest in writing grew. He was awarded 2nd place in the National Capital Youth Writing Competition in 2013. He continues to explore various approaches to writing alongside pursuing his other passion, aviation. An active member of the flying community, he has been repeatedly recognized for his dedication, enthusiasm, and professionalism in his craft.

www.ingramcontent.com/pod-product-compliance
Lightning Source LLC
Chambersburg PA
CBHW020755130626
46554CB00006B/2191